Jace Wins the Race

JESSICA K. CHILDERS

Illustrated by Nafisa Arshad

LUMINARE PRESS
WWW.LUMINAREPRESS.COM

Jace Wins the Race

Printed in the United States of America

Luminare Press
442 Charnelton St.
Eugene, OR 97401
www.luminarepress.com

LCCN: 2021919841
ISBN: 978-1-64388-833-0

To all my readers, thank you for taking an interest in my first book. I would like to thank my beautiful wife, Latosha, for encouraging me and supporting me in all my endeavors.

Special thanks to my mother and sister for believing in me since day one. To my children, Shanise, Rae, and Jace, you are my motivation. I hope this book makes you proud.

I dedicate this book to my late, loving grandmother, Ruby Wilson.

HELLO

"Wake up, wake up, wake up! It is time for school, and today's the big day."

"Mom, ten more minutes," Jace says as he places his pillow over his face, hiding from his mother.

"Nice try! You have five minutes to get downstairs so we can eat breakfast and head to school." She playfully grabs the pillow and bops him on the head. "Also, remember to pack your new running shoes for track tryouts today."

Jace squints his eyes, glances at the shoes, and shakes his head. "Mom, I would rather run barefoot."

Quickly, his mom says, "Jace I know you wanted those expensive, walk-on-the-clouds, fancy-pants shoes, but these are quality shoes at a bargain price. Get over it!"

"By *bargain* you mean *cheap*, right?" Jace responds with a salty stare.

"Four minutes, smarty pants."

12 1 2 3 4 5 6 7 8 9 10 11
HELLO

After school that day, Jace heads down to the track. Nervously, he whispers to himself, "I really hope I don't make a fool of myself today. I mean, I am not even that fast. What am I thinking? I should just wait another year."

His friend Rae runs up playfully behind him and nudges him. "Are you ready for tryouts?"

"Not really," he says. "I am so nervous."

"And to top it all, my mom bought me these lame shoes for tryouts. Ugh! What am I supposed to do in these? I specifically asked her for the new Turbo Elites, and she got me these." Jace frowns. Just as Jace and Rae look down at his shoes, the class superstar, Liam, walks up. He has on the new white and red Turbo Elites with the matching shirt and shorts.

Jace's and Rae's jaws drop in awe. "I'm *doomed*," Jace mumbles under his breath. Everyone surrounds Liam, admiring his fresh look. "Rae, look at him. He looks like he has rockets on his feet. He is going to smoke me."

"So what? His shoes look cool. Well, his whole outfit looks cool, but what matters is talent. He may dress the part, but does he have the talent to win? You have to try. They're only shoes," Rae reminds Jace.

"Phwwwwwhht!" Coach Brooks's whistle blows. "All right runners and tryout participants, make your way to the track. It is time to get to work!" she yells. As Jace and the other runners make their way to the start line of the track, Liam's laughter gains Jace's attention.

He turns around and notices Liam laughing and mocking his shoes. “Hey man, where did you get those shoes?” Liam says with an overconfident smirk. “What are those, the new Turbo Deflates?” With everyone staring and giggling, Jace hangs his head.

Jace attempts to walk off, but Rae stops him. "Jace, you cannot quit. You are one of the fastest dudes I know. Do not let his corny jokes get in the way of you trying out. Have confidence in your speed."

"He is going to smoke me. These stupid shoes have already embarrassed me enough. My shoes are wack!" Jace shouts in anger.

Frustrated, Rae responds, “So your shoes suck because they don’t have a fancy name like his shoes? Dude, you’re bigger than something as simple as a pair of shoes. Is this a fashion show or a tryout for the track team?”

Convinced, Jace takes a deep breath and agrees. He slowly approaches the start line. As he stretches and bends down to get set, he can still see Liam laughing and looking at his shoes. Liam then tightens his Turbo straps and whispers to Jace, "Take a picture of my back." He snickers. Jace tunes him out and gets in race position.

"Runners, on your mark, get set, GOOOOOOO!" Coach Brooks yells. Jace and Liam both get off to a great start. As the runners sprint down the track, Jace glances over and notices that he and Liam are neck and neck. Both boys pump their arms and take long strides down the track.

Jace can hear Rae's voice near the finish line. "You got this, Jace. You're too fast." With less than twenty meters to go, Jace remembers Liam's pointing and mocking. His adrenaline kicks in, and he takes off. With his intense boost, he takes the lead and crosses the finish line. He scans his surroundings and realizes he won.

Soon, the other runners start to cross the finish line. Rae runs toward Jace, proudly clapping. "Hey man, you were amazing, lightning fast."

Coach Brooks approaches Jace and announces, "Welcome to the team, Jace, you're going to do great things." With a huge smile on his face, Jace responds, "Thank you so much, Coach."

"There is no way. I can't believe I did not win," Liam whines. He fiddles with the gadgets on his shoes.

Jace approaches Liam. "Hey, good race."

Feeling embarrassed and ashamed, Liam answers, "Thanks, and congrats on the win and making the team."

"You got skills," Jace says encouragingly to Liam. "Just rely on your speed instead of your shoes next time."

Liam smirks and laughs. "You got that right. Clearly these shoes are more for show then performance. I may just have to get me some like yours."

Jace walks off with a bounce in his step. "Hey, they got the job done today."

The End.

Jessica was born and raised in Hallandale Beach, Florida. Growing up, she was a five-star athlete. A graduate of Florida State University, she is currently a special education specialist. After recently becoming a new mom, she ventured off to write a book with her son as the main character. From working with students, she knows firsthand the types of peer pressure they experience. She wrote this book in the hope that it gives students confidence in their abilities.

Made in the USA
Coppell, TX
06 April 2024